FESTIVAL ™

By
CHRISTOPHER GOLDEN
and TIM LEBBON

Cover and Illustrations by
PETER BERGTING

Dark Horse Books

President and Publisher
MIKE RICHARDSON

Editor
KATII O'BRIEN

Associate Editor
JENNY BLENK

Assistant Editor
MISHA GEHR

Designer
MAY HIJIKURO

Digital Art Technician
BETSY HOWITT

Published by Dark Horse Books®
A division of Dark Horse Comics LLC
10956 SE Main St, Milwaukie, Or 97222
www.darkhorse.com

First edition October 2022
ISBN: 978-1-50673-229-9 | eBook ISBN 978-1-50673-212-1

10 9 8 7 6 5 4 3 2 1
Printed in China

Library of Congress Cataloging-in-Publication Data

Names: Golden, Christopher, author. | Lebbon, Tim, author. | Bergting,
  Peter, illustrator.
Title: Festival / by Christopher Golden and Tim Lebbon ; cover and
  illustrations by Peter Bergting.
Description: First edition. | Milwaukie, OR : Dark Horse Books, 2022. |
  Summary: "The Valhalla music festival commemorates a long-ago Viking
  slaughter, but when strange things start to happen it seems the massacre
  may be far from over. When festival-goers begin to disappear, and
  musicians find themselves playing mysterious and ancient songs as if
  possessed, the fans have to figure out what's going on before the
  festival site's haunting past comes back for blood!"-- Provided by
  publisher.
Identifiers: LCCN 2022014162 (print) | LCCN 2022014163 (ebook) | ISBN
  9781506732299 (hardcover) | ISBN 9781506732121 (ebook)
Subjects: LCSH: Music festivals--Fiction. | LCGFT: Horror fiction. |
  Novels.
Classification: LCC PS3557.035927 F47 2022 (print) | LCC PS3557.035927
  (ebook) | DDC 813/.54--dc23/eng/20220506
LC record available at https://lccn.loc.gov/2022014162
LC ebook record available at https://lccn.loc.gov/2022014163

CHAPTER 1 ◆ PIPPA

She felt the drums in her chest, as if the music had replaced her heart. The guitars clanged and cried, but only the drums carried up the hill and through the trees with the same volume—the same urgency—they had down on the festival grounds.

"It's like you can't hide from them, even if you wanted to," Kev said, glancing back down the trail. He reached for Pippa's hand and she took it, steadied herself.

"Hide from what?"

"The drums," Kev said. "Surely you feel it."

Pippa smiled. One of the things she loved about Kev was the way he always seemed so perfectly attuned to her own feelings. What did they call that? An empath? Whatever the name for it, Kev had a gift—at least with her. He could put words to things she had only been thinking, as if he'd plucked them from her mind. *Simpatico*. Was that the word?

It worked that way in bed, too. At nineteen, Pippa had only been with two other guys, but based on her limited experience with the fumbling hands and inexpert tongues of Corain and Rob, she thought she ought to stick with Kev forever.

"I do," she said, smiling to her-self at the implications of the phrase when she'd been thinking about Kev and forever. You're just *nineteen*, her mum said every time she caught Pippa with a familiar moony smile on her face.

Mum was right. Always right. But the way Kev made Pippa feel, it was hard to think about a future without him in it.

"I was thinking the same thing," she said. "It's like the distance and the trees muffle all the other instruments but the drum gets through. Like the hills and the forest open for the drums because they're ancient, cuz they know the beat of a drum."

Kev smiled, that mischievous grin that always did her in. "There's my poet."

Pippa blushed a bit. She wrote poetry, knew she'd never be great and even if she might be, she'd never make a living off it. Instead, she intended to teach literature and hoped to do well enough to get the upper level kids. Last thing she wanted to do was oversee a bunch of unruly hooligans every day.

She had another yearning, a secret ambition she hadn't even shared with Kev, no matter how simpatico they might be. His stepsister Ellie, just sixteen, had already started a band. The girl had a voice like a raging angel, and her mate Lenore played guitar like one of the prodigies always showing up on social media. One of their video clips had gone halfway viral last autumn. Ellie wrote most of their tunes, but her lyrics were often shit. Pippa might be three years their elder, but it was taking her a lot to work up the nerve to show Ellie and Lenore some of her poems-that-might-be-lyrics.

A little luck, and she'd earn a hell of a lot more writing songs than teaching poetry to blank young faces.

"There she goes, off with the fairies."

Pippa blinked. They'd continued walking up the trail, lost in the shade of the trees on either side of the path, but she couldn't have said how her feet had kept moving. Kev liked to tease her about being a dreamer, her mind wandering far ahead of her feet. This time, though, he smiled as if she were the gift he'd asked Santa for, pulled her close, and kissed her.

She gave a little hum of delight and then broke off the kiss. "You think that's going to help me focus?"

Kev laughed and took her hand, guiding the way up the trail. They'd come up here looking for the Wednesday Tree, ostensibly. Pippa had a feeling their trip into the woods would end up with the two of them shagging somewhere a bit too close to the trail for real privacy, and the idea sent a little tingle through her.

So it surprised her a bit when, not five minutes later, Kev tugged her hand and led her off the path, down a narrow rutted trail so steep and criss-crossed with exposed tree roots that it looked more like a ladder, and into the small glade that surrounded the Wednesday Tree.

The drumbeat kept up its rhythm. Down on the festival grounds, the band had moved onto their next song, but the drums seemed somehow independent now, as if the song no longer mattered. As if the primal beat that thrummed in the trees and in the ground underfoot was something the hills gave up to them now, echoes from another time.

The poet, she thought to herself. *Always trying to make magic out of everyday bullshit.*

Kev had picked her up just after eight a.m. and presented her with an iced coffee and a chocolate donut. They'd be meeting up with his family later, but there'd been no room in the family caravan for them, which suited Pippa perfectly. She loved Kev's family, but wanted to keep at least a little of this adventure just for the two of them. It would be nice later on to share the family's picnic blankets and food and beer and of course the music. Kev's mum, Zoe, had a warm and shining heart that made Pippa feel loved. Her wife, Jasmine, could be a bit high-strung but Pippa loved the woman's no-bullshit approach to life.

The first time Pippa had met Kev's family, she'd felt a bit awkward, but his mums had instantly dispelled her nerves. She'd known plenty of gay people, of course, but this clan were unique in her experience. Kev's mum Zoe had been a single mother, the dad nowhere to be found, and Ellie's mum Jasmine had gotten a divorce after falling in love with a woman for the first time. The love that filled their house felt almost like magic. Sure, Zoe and Jasmine butted heads with their kids the way any parent might, but there was joy in Kev's house that Pippa envied. She didn't think Kev and Ellie even realized how lucky they were.

Now she glanced at Kev, reached out and took his hand and smiled at her good fellow, grateful for the women who'd made him that way.

Kev had turned to look down the hill, back through the trees toward the festival grounds, but at the touch of her hand he looked back at Pippa.

"It's gone quiet," he said.

From up here they could only see the makeshift roof that hung over the festival's main stage. The trees blocked out the crowds and any sign of the two smaller stages, never mind the fields turned into carparks just off the narrow road that led from the local village up to Valhalla Hill. The village economy had seen a hell of a boost this year thanks to the run-up to the Valhalla Music Festival. The U.K. had so many music festivals at this point there didn't seem room for another, but the organizers had found an obscure bit of local history to pin this one on. If Pippa understood properly, it involved the millennial anniversary of a mass homicide, which sort of killed the romance for her. But with Billie Eilish, Post Malone, Flogging Molly, Frank Turner, and a miraculously preserved The Cure all on the same bill, it was going to be the festival of the fucking year, so she could forgive a little genocidal slaughter.

Vikings, she thought it had been. Or something. Kev would know. They were simpatico.

The music had indeed fallen silent down below. One of the secondary stages would be kicking into gear in a moment. This early on the first day, it'd only be warmup acts, even on the main stage, so she didn't feel like they were missing anything. Besides, they'd wanted to see the Wednesday Tree.

Pippa gave a little laugh and popped the heel of her hand against her forehead. "I'm slow on the uptake."

Kev slid his arms around her, smiled as he kissed her. "How's that?"

"I've just worked it out, haven't I? Ever since you read that bit to me from the festival website, I figured yeah, we'll go up and look at the spooky old tree. Viking rituals, blah blah blah. But I only just put it together. The Wednesday Tree. Wednesday's named after Odin—Woden, they called him—king of the Asgardian gods."

"Norse gods."

"Anthony Hopkins played him in the movies," Pippa went on. "But there's a story about Odin being tied to a tree, or nailed to it like Christ on the cross or something, yeah?"

"That's it, yeah," Kev replied. "Though I doubt anyone's saying this is the same tree. Just that there were Vikings here once upon a time, and maybe they worshipped Odin here. Sacrificed goats to him, or the people who pissed them off."

Pippa reached toward him without looking and he took her hand, the both of them studying the ancient tree. A little chill went through her, which she knew had more to do with the shade of the massive, sprawling canopy

of the tree, but if anyone suggested she might also be more than a little un-
nerved she wouldn't have called them a liar. There were thousands of places
like this, forested hills cut through with ancient footpaths where the quiet

shade made the land feel haunted. Pippa had hiked and walked her share of such trails, but never encountered a tree quite like this.

The massive stone beneath it could easily have been an altar in the time of the Druids. The altar stone had been there longer than the tree, but through some miracle of nature's determination, it had grown on top of the rock, massive roots spread across the stone and spilling over the sides like the wax of a melted candle. The base of the trunk must have been eight feet across, the bark gnarled and runneled with age. As it had grown, the tree had split off into multiple trunks—she counted four—which allowed the dense crown of leaves to give the glade the feeling of a secret place.

"Spooky," Kev said. Squeezing her hand, he released her and walked over to a plaque on a post that jutted from the earth a few feet from the Wednesday Tree.

"Beautiful, though," she murmured. Pippa still felt that chill, but the tree ignited her imagination.

Kev turned from the plaque with a grin. "You're already composing a poem about it, aren't you?"

She tilted her head, smiling shyly. "Mayyyyyyybe." Or maybe a song.

A fresh drumbeat kicked in, carrying up through the trees from the festival stage. She hesitated, listening closely to make sure it wasn't Post Malone. He weren't supposed to perform until tonight, but she wouldn't put it past him to come out and do a short set early on, when the crowd was still gathering. In the distance, someone began to sing. The words were unintelligible from so far away, but she could tell the voice belonged to a woman, and she relaxed.

"You should read this, babe." Kev glanced back at her, gesturing toward the plaque. "There's a ton of lore about the tree."

Pippa walked up to the tree, studying the deeply grooved bark. She reached out to run her hand along it. "We read about it. All the Odin stuff."

"There's more," he said, then began to read aloud. "'Many local legends have sprung up over the centuries regarding the Wednesday Tree, also called . . . ' something in Welsh I can't read. 'Early in the 16th century, the family of Perkin Warbeck settled nearby. Warbeck impersonated the murdered son of Richard III and was executed for his pretence in 1499. Twenty-five years later, his son (also Perkin) and daughter-in-law Catherine visited the Wednesday Tree. The younger Perkin reported that locals informed his wife that if she walked widdershins round the tree three times, she could visit the fairies.'"

"Oh, let me guess," Pippa said, leaning against the altar and the tree's roots. "His wife mysteriously vanished in the fucking woods and poor Perkin just didn't know what to do with himself?"

"Why, darling, is that sarcasm I detect?"

Pippa rolled her eyes and turned to run her fingers along the tree bark again. "So much easier for abusive men to rid themselves of their girlfriends and wives in those days. 'Oh, she walked widdershins around an ugly bloody tree and, poof! Off with the fairies!'"

"You think Warbeck Junior killed his bride?" Kev asked, pondering.

The drums down the hill thumped through the trees. She felt the rhythm in her chest, in her bones and blood. Pippa wanted to dance.

"'Course he did. Here, let's see," she said, beginning to rock with the music.

Pippa swayed her hips, let her shoulders roll with the beat. She trailed her fingers along the rough bark as she began to circle the Wednesday Tree and its altar. Each time she went round, still moving to the music, she bared a bit of skin, casting Kev the sort of glances she knew would tug at the primal part of him, enjoying the expression on his face each time. The second time round the Wednesday Tree, she snickered a bit while flashing a bit of lacy bra, unable to take herself seriously.

The third time around, of course, she didn't emerge at all.

CHAPTER 2 ✦ JOSHUA

Joshua hated being late for anything, and now he was running across fields, summer crops whipping at his bare legs, sweat sticking his tee shirt to his skinny torso, guitar case banging against his back and straps chafing his shoulder. The biggest gig of his life was due to start in a little under half an hour and he was *going to fucking miss it.*

He'd abandoned his old clapped-out car twenty minutes earlier. He'd pulled out of the traffic queue and tucked his car into a field gateway, almost certain that some angry farmer would shift it with a tractor later today or tomorrow. Equally certain that it had to be done. If he'd sat and waited in the traffic queue he'd definitely have missed his set, and Frank had told him he'd come to watch. Frank fucking Turner, man!

At least now he had a chance. Panting, he regretted the heavy smoking habit of his twenties, the days and nights lost to pot and acid in his thirties, and the drinking he still enjoyed now, well into his forties. He bemoaned his constant desire to get fit and continued excuses as to why he didn't have time.

I'm never smoking again, he thought as breath rasped in and out of his lungs. It had been a long, hot, dry summer, and the air abraded his throat. *I'm never drinking . . .* Well, maybe that was going a little too far. He paused and took a swig of single malt from his hip flask. It thinned the blood, didn't it? He'd seen Eddie Izzard taking drams from supporters along the way while he was running his thirty marathons in thirty days, hadn't he?

Besides, Valhalla was close. He'd been able to hear it the moment he'd left his car, a constant, distant thumping of drums. He could almost feel it through the ground, and through a vibration deep in his chest. Now, as he got closer he could smell the festival, too, and it smelled like comfort, peace, and contentment. The miasma of familiar scents always calmed him and made him feel at home—the stale warmth of seventy thousand unwashed bodies, the tang of smoke from fires and joints, spilled alcohol, cooking food, and the smell of humanity having a great time. To Joshua, a musician, it was music that always instilled the most powerful memories. But carried on the still summer air, the aroma of Valhalla Festival lured him on and gave him strength.

He started to run again.

The road curved around the long, low, wooded hill that bordered the western edge of the festival site—the hill known to locals and villagers as Valhalla, and which had given the festival its name—but Joshua decided to go up and over. He thought it might get him to the small stage quicker, and he relished the chance to be in amongst that ancient woodland, climbing and descending through the trees. He'd lost count of how many times he had visited this place, and he couldn't wait to see what the vast festival site would look like sprawled across the countryside. Even though he'd been born over a hundred miles away, whenever Joshua approached the village just to the south and its surrounding hills, it felt like coming home.

He climbed a farm gate and found himself in a field of brambles and nettles. He paused, and stillness fell around him. For a moment his heart kept time with the distant thump of drums, and the hot summer air was utterly motionless, clasping him in a furnace fist. He'd be soaked with sweat before he even stepped onto the stage, and that made him self-conscious, and worried what people would think of him.

I'll forget about it as soon as I strum the first chord, he thought. *Once the music takes me, I'll forget about everything. The sweaty clothes. The tiredness. This fucking headache.* He looked to the far side of the wild field where the trees and hill began. *And the stings and scratches will just be another part of the show.*

Shrugging his guitar into a more comfortable position, he pushed his way across the field. Nettles kissed his bare shins and calves and left their familiar tingling sensation behind, soon to develop into a more painful itch. Brambles reached out and gave him pale scratches that quickly beaded blood. He raised his hands above his head instead of using them to push plants aside, because his music was born through his fingers. His throat and mouth, too, but he was renowned for his gruff voice. When he strapped on his guitar it was his fingers that really sang.

He reached the edge of the field and started up the slope onto Valhalla Hill. Trees welcomed him in, their cool, timeless embrace so familiar, though he hadn't been here for nearly ten months thanks to the patchwork tour of Europe he'd been on. Joshua and several other working musicians had traveled the continent in a seventeen-year-old bus, playing impromptu sets at town halls, university campuses, and clubs, as well as fulfilling a series of dubious bookings his so-called agent occasionally arranged for him.

Now he welcomed the shadowy cover of the old trees, the whisper and rustle of leaves even though the hot air was heavy and dead, the steady thump-thump of the festival beyond the hill sounding like a frantic heart-beat, and the smells of the forest. He'd been to a hundred woodlands in his lifetime, maybe more, but none of them felt like Valhalla. To him, this place had always been like getting to heaven and finding out it was exactly how you'd pictured in your head.

As he climbed, the sounds and scents of the festival grew more prevalent and powerful. The guitar on his back felt lighter even though he was moving uphill, as though it was eager to start playing. Music took him to heights that were difficult to attain by other means, even drink or drugs. Even sex.

The Wednesday Tree was not far away. He smiled, as he always did when he thought of that strange place, the ancient oak growing around and across that weird stone slab that many said had once been a sacrificial altar. He'd visited the tree a dozen times, in all seasons of the year, during the day and at night, but it was his first time there that always brought a smile, because it had been an evening of first times. Her name had been Maddy Woodham, and she'd lured him onto the hill, into the woods, and to the base of the tree with a promise of intimate wonders. She'd teased him along for hours, turning this way and that up and around the hill, and they'd fooled around and taken swigs from the bottles of Thunderbird wine each of them carried. By the time they reached the tree, Joshua's

drunkenness had been purged by his desire. She had splayed back on the altar against the base of the tree, and guided him in. The loss of his virginity would have been unremarkable were it not for their surroundings—the tree shushed and whispered in the evening breeze, moonlight filtered down through the canopy, and Maddy's pale skin seemed to glow with borrowed starlight. He'd only seen her one more time after that, but she lived bright in his memory forever.

Especially today, this close to the tree. He would visit it again sometime during the festival, and spend a few moments in fond recollection of his first night and first time there. But not right now.

As he reached a low ridge, and the main festival site became visible through the trees, he heard someone running towards him. Footsteps pounded across the uneven forest floor, leaves crunching, sticks snapping, and Joshua felt a brief but rich moment of fear and dread. His heart stuttered and he spun around to face the wild-eyed young guy racing toward him.

"Have you seen her?" the young man asked.

"Wait. What?"

The man skidded to a stop, kicking up a storm of dust and twigs.

"She went. She was there, then she was gone. Have you seen her? Pippa?"

"I don't know a Pippa. What's happened?"

"We went for a walk, we were going to . . . " The young man looked around, eyes never still, breath ragged and panicked. He looked fit but his voice sounded sick with worry, and his skin was pale, slick. Joshua wondered if he'd been taking something.

"I haven't seen a girl," Joshua said. "I haven't seen anyone. I'm late for the festival, got a gig, and I'm late. I've got to—"

"She went around the tree one more time and never came out the other side." He was frowning now, staring past Joshua into the trees. Almost talking to himself, as if to make sense of something that had happened, or perhaps hadn't happened at all.

"Okay, hang on now, what's your name?"

"Kev. Kev."

"You having a bad trip, friend?"

Kev looked at him. "Fucking, no. No. I've had a drink, and Pippa had one too. And now she's gone."

"Wait, what tree?" Joshua asked.

"Big tree on a rock."

"The Wednesday Tree."

"You haven't seen her," Kev said, and he ran past Joshua and downhill towards the festival.

"Well," Joshua said. "Guess I should run too."

He followed Kev, soon losing sight of him but still being drawn down through the trees towards the sprawling, bustling, colourful and insanely beautiful Valhalla Festival. By the time he left the forest and crossed a dusty, thronged car park towards one of the several entrances, his strange encounter with Kev, and his memories of clumsy lust beneath the Wednesday Tree, were all but forgotten. He had his mind on other things, and his guitar was ready to sing. Here he was. Valhalla. Home.

Before the day was out, he would think of that strange, ancient tree again. And he would wish it had never cast its roots through the memories of his life.

CHAPTER 3 ◆ LENORE

Lenore might have been a little bit in love with Ellie. If she was being honest, she'd have to admit she'd been feeling that way ever since stumbling into an impromptu gig Ellie had put on for her friends from St. James School. Lenore had been dragged along by Albert Lloyd, a boy who'd been desperate to take things beyond the occasional snog.

The gig had been a drowsy Sunday morning in the back garden of a pub that wouldn't open for hours yet. Ellie perched on the stone wall with a Martin acoustic guitar that looked like a relic from another age. She had elfin features—pointed chin, narrow nose, ghostly blue eyes—and wore her hair tied back in a no-fucks-to-give ponytail. She sang "Blackbird" and then Springsteen's "Growin' Up" in a voice that sounded like a magic trick, meant to make you hers forever.

It had worked on Lenore.

They'd been fourteen years old at the time.

The strange part was that, aside from Ellie, Lenore had never felt anything for another girl except some combination of camaraderie and disdain, on a sliding scale dependent on her mood. She mostly liked boys. Now that she'd reached the ripe old age of seventeen, she occasionally liked men instead of boys. Lenore had obliged Albert Lloyd that night three years before—beyond his wildest dreams. There had been a lot of whiskey and Guinness and a little bit of smoke, and listening to Ellie had her feeling good, so she'd snatched his virginity away and then had to deal with him fussing over her and sniffing after her until she moved up into sixth form.

There'd been other boys. As of this morning, Lenore had been with Rob Guilfoyle for six months. She liked him well enough, enjoyed the

sex, liked to laugh with him, and Rob never minded playing roadie when the band had a gig. Best thing about Rob Guilfoyle, though, was that he understood where he stood on her priority list—below the music, and the band, and definitely below Ellie. When Lenore had told him she was headed off to Valhalla Festival with Ellie's family, Rob hadn't batted an eyelash. No whinging about not being invited along, her not being around for their six month anniversary, nothing of the sort. Lenore would keep him around for a while.

Ellie, though . . . Ellie had her hooked for life.

"Get you anything, love? Jasmine made scones. I know you love her strawberry jam."

Lenore shook herself from her reverie. They were between sets now. Ellie had been squired off a dozen feet or so by her mum, Jasmine. Lenore had been sitting back on the blanket she and Ellie were sharing while Jasmine's wife, Zoe, unpacked things from their basket. There'd been a lot of alcohol dragged onto the festival grounds, but thermoses of coffee and cartons and coolers of food as well. They were well-prepared.

"Go on, then," Lenore said, scooting across the blanket to join Zoe on hers.

Zoe hadn't waited for her to agree before beginning to prepare a scone for her. Coffee seemed a grand idea as well. Most of the people around them had already dipped into their stores of whiskey and beer, but Lenore liked the homey quality of time spent with Ellie's family. Her own home life often seemed a parody of some pitiful BBC drama, father unable to keep a job, mum always prickly, convinced she'd married beneath her station. They hated each other with such ferocity that they only seemed to remember they'd even had a daughter when they were drunk enough that they could no longer outrun the monstrous regret that constantly chased them both.

But at least Lenore had music.

Music . . . and Ellie's family. Even the flirty teasing Lenore took from Ellie's stepbrother Kev felt warm and cozy and loving most of the time. That was how deep her craving for normalcy went. Everyone else—anyone who wasn't a part of Ellie's family—got Lenore's resting punk face. A sneer from beneath thick black eyeliner and the nest of dirty blond curls that often obscured her eyes. Other girls tended to love her hair, and hate that the only thing she did to get the look was wash it twice a week.

At gigs, Lenore drew all the right attention. On stage, she was magnetic and she knew it, but on the street people gave her a wide berth and she liked it that way.

Lenore glanced over at Ellie and her mum again. She could tell by the way the two had their spines straightened that they were disagreeing. Did they realize how much they mirrored one another? Lenore thought not, and doubted Ellie would appreciate the observation. The girl loved her mum, but wanted to pave her own road.

A beach ball spun overhead, floating as if it had a bit of helium inside. A hand reached up from the crowd and batted it the opposite direction. Lenore watched it bounce amongst the crowd. The wonderful buzz of the festival enveloped her and she felt at home in its embrace. Laughter and voices, distant music, the susurrus of anticipation for this band or that, the smells of a hundred spices drifting from the food tents or from baskets packed for the occasion. Simply being in the presence of so many joyful people at one time felt intoxicating.

"Here you go, love," Zoe said, handing over a paper plate with Lenore's scone. She was such a nurturing mother that it often made Lenore jealous. Did Ellie realize how fortunate she was to have two strong, loving women to raise her when Lenore herself only had a cold, emotional vacuum shaped like a grown woman?

Lenore envied Ellie almost as much as she loved her.

They were bandmates, and best mates, but so far they had never even flirted with the idea of being more. Lenore wasn't sure if she'd even like sex with another girl, but though she'd never admit it to anyone but herself, she knew she would be whatever Ellie wanted her to be, as long as it meant they would always be together. Always stay close.

"Coffee?" Zoe asked.

"Yes, thanks," Lenore replied. When Zoe opened the thermos, she smelled the rich coffee scent and halfway went to heaven. "You're the consummate mum."

Zoe sat cross-legged on her own blanket and poured Lenore a cup of coffee. The sun shone down and the breeze brought the rich scent of earth and trees. Music drifted to them from the smaller stage, southwest of where they'd laid out their blankets, but the main stage had gone quiet as crew members moved amps and instruments around. Go Betty Go had just wrapped a forty minute set and would play again tomorrow. There'd also been a rumour that Alicia Keys might have flown over to attend the festival and would get on stage with Billie Eilish tonight for "Ocean Eyes." Lenore preferred moshing to Mongol Horde and was looking forward to Post Malone, who'd play last tonight. But she planned to enjoy every minute, every song.

"Here we are!" a voice sang out.

Lenore glanced up to see Nathaniel emerge from the crowd. He was Zoe and Jasmine's dearest mate, a perpetually single gay bloke from the cycling club Zoe belonged to. Right now Nathaniel was beaming with pride and laden with festival merchandise. Lenore always tried to support the merch tables at small shows by musicians struggling to make a career, but she'd be damned if she'd put what little money she had into the pockets of the festival itself. Later on, she intended to head to the second stage and haunt the merch tables there, where bands like Rust Bucket and Autumn Deering were hawking their wares.

Nathaniel had no such self-imposed restrictions. He was a bearded, amiably middle-aged mathematics teacher, just happy to be out of the house and part of this wonderful clan who had adopted him as a brother and uncle and friend. The punk in her knew she ought to disdain a man as cheerful as Nathaniel, but he was so kind she couldn't manage it.

As if to reinforce her thoughts, Nathaniel crouched beside her and unfurled a black t-shirt with a showman's flourish. This particular Valhalla Festival shirt had a scratchy sketch silhouette of an axe-wielding Viking warrior being run through with a spear.

"I know you don't go for the real commercial merch," Nathaniel said, smiling thinly, "but I thought you might make an exception for this."

Lenore took the offered shirt and for a moment could only stare at it. She liked it—a lot—but what struck her the most was the gesture. Her own parents wouldn't have done this for her, never mind reading her well enough to know what she would or wouldn't like.

Nathaniel looked uncertain. "Was I wrong?"

"God, no. It's just . . . you shouldn't have done it."

"I wanted to," he said. "You save your money to support the starving artists. But I saw that and thought, 'well, Lenore'll like *that* one, and then she'll have a souvenir to remember the day.'"

Lenore's eyes burned, felt a bit itchy, and it took her a second to realize she might be about to cry. The knowledge made her laugh instead and she stood up and gave Nathaniel a little hug.

"It's really sweet of you. Thank you."

The moment might've turned slightly awkward, but then Zoe asked if he wanted coffee or scones and Nathaniel declined, choosing instead to open the cooler and pull out a beer. He'd bought a Valhalla Festival blanket as well, and now he unfurled it and managed to overlap with the other two in a way that didn't infuriate the festival-goers around them.

Zoe picked up the cup Lenore had left nestled on her blanket and handed it over.

As Lenore sipped her coffee, new t-shirt clutched in the other hand, the music kicked in on the main stage and she realized Stormzy had come on. The lineup for Valhalla was eclectic as hell. Later in the afternoon FKA Twigs and Father John Misty were scheduled to play a short set together. Lenore didn't consider herself a Stormzy fan, but the atmosphere was contagious and she bounced along to the thumping beat.

Then Ellie pushed through the crowd, a scowl on her face and her mum trailing behind her looking sad.

"Come for a walk," Ellie said, grabbing Lenore's arm.

"Where are we—"

Ellie tugged at her, sweeping Lenore away from the blankets. Coffee spilled from her cup, splashed a bit on her new t-shirt. Lenore wanted to bark at her, but when Ellie was this upset it would only make things worse. *Temperamental artists*, she thought with a wistful smile.

They were thirty feet away, behind a cluster of people who were jumping in place, hands in the air for Stormzy, when Ellie finally let her go. Lenore dumped the rest of her coffee and waited, but she didn't have to wait long.

"She's such a bitch!" Ellie threw her hands up, shook her head, turned in a bit of a circle as if she wanted to do some more stomping about but couldn't decide where to go. "What's she think, she runs my life? She can just spring something like this on me and I'll go along with it? I'm not ready. I'll only humiliate myself and in front of this crowd that'd be the end of things. It'd be over before things got started for us, Lenore."

Ellie hung her head and started cursing as if the dirt beneath their feet were her worst enemy.

Lenore grabbed her wrist. "Ellie."

She hadn't shouted, but Ellie knew the tone.

"My mum's trying to do something nice," Ellie explained. "I know she meant well, but—"

"You said 'in front of this crowd,'" Lenore reminded her, staring. Her heart thumped a bit harder as she locked eyes with Ellie. "You telling me your mum thinks she can get you on the stage?"

Ellie exhaled, calming down as Lenore spoke. Then she nodded. "Yeah. But just me. Not the band. Not you, Lenore."

"That doesn't matter!" Lenore stared at her. "*How*, exactly?"

"Turns out my mums have a friend who's a friend of Frank Turner's tour manager, who played him that video of us at Muhazzim's party—"

"We were drunk on the bloody patio. We were crap!"

Ellie shrugged. "Apparently he liked my voice."

"'Course he did. You're a fucking angel. But we were crap."

Thoughts tumbled through her head. Maybe her playing had been crap that night, and even Ellie's guitar had sounded awful, but her voice—gods, her voice. Lenore tossed her new t-shirt over her shoulder and reached both hands out to steady Ellie, holding her face, eyes locked.

"You saying to me that your mums have got a way to get you up on that stage and you've told them no?"

"She only just told me, didn't she? I can't go up there cold."

"Your mum's set up what'll like be the biggest opportunity of your life— for you *and* for the band—and you're stomping about having a tantrum?"

Ellie winced, had the decency to shoot a guilty look at the ground. "What would I even do?"

Lenore laughed, pulled her close and kissed her forehead, then whispered in her ear. "You'd do whatever Frank Turner wants you to do."

In a very small voice, Ellie said, "He liked my cover of 'Creep.' When I did it like the Tori Amos version."

Lenore could barely breathe. Frank Turner had liked the shitty video of Ellie singing at Muhazzim's party enough that he'd chased up other videos of her. Of them, the band. Now he wanted her to get up on stage at the Valhalla Festival in front of thousands of people and do it live.

"You're getting up on that stage," Lenore said.

Ellie seemed about to argue. A shadow passed across her face, but then she exhaled and a little smile replaced it.

"I know."

Lenore almost kissed her.

Might have, if Kev hadn't nearly knocked them over right then. He was crying, and Kev did not cry. Not ever.

"She's gone!" he said, looking from Lenore to Ellie. "Pippa's gone! Just . . . just vanished!"

Lenore frowned, but it was Ellie who put voice to the thought in both their heads.

"Who the fuck is Pippa?"

CHAPTER 4 ◆ JASMINE

"So who the fuck is Pippa?" Jasmine whispered in Zoe's ear.

"Beats me."

Kev had slumped onto the blankets, and now Zoe knelt and put her hand on her son's shoulder. She shook, trying to grab his attention, and his head lolled on his neck before he seemed to come around and look at her. His vacant gaze sent a chill through Jasmine.

Oh shit please don't have taken something, Jasmine thought. *Not now, not here and so close to Ellie's big moment. Don't fuck it up for her.*

Jasmine moved toward her wife and stepson, bent and kissed Kev's head, and then backed away. She wanted them both to know she was here for them, but to let them work this out—whatever *this* was—on their own.

Zoe's Kev was a good kid. He and Jasmine's daughter, Ellie, got on just fine. They'd become siblings when their mums decided to get married, but they had also become friends. Ellie had told Jasmine that Kev had once assured her they'd have been mates even if they hadn't been "made to be brother and sister." Ellie had brushed it off as if it were nothing, but Jasmine knew she wouldn't have shared at all if it hadn't meant a great deal to her.

It had been sweet, and both mums had taken real comfort from that. But Jasmine could never quite put out of her mind the fact Kev had drug demons in his past. He'd been steady and apparently clean for at least two years, but none of them could forget the midnight phone calls from concerned friends and, once, the local police. The times spent talking to him and supporting him and nursing him through bad nights. As stepmum, Jasmine had done all she could to be a positive force, a guiding hand for Kev, even when Zoe had been beside herself with worry.

As a family, they'd pulled together and moved through that dark period and out the other side. There'd been no repeats of those more dangerous, traumatic episodes, but they had been on edge for days about bringing Kev into an environment such as this, especially letting him drive his own car. They'd smelled the pot from the moment they approached the Festival's eastern gate, and Zoe had been eager to meet up with Kev. Messages to his phone remained unanswered, although reception here was poor.

This wasn't quite the reunion Jasmine had been hoping for.

Don't you fuck up my girl's big chance, she thought. It was unfair, a thought she would never verbalize, one of those interior dialogues that took no notice of niceties. But she couldn't help it.

A hand touched Jasmine's arm. It was Ellie, with Lenore just a step behind her.

"Mum," said Ellie quietly. "What's happened to him?"

Jasmine didn't know how to answer. The argument she'd just had with Ellie vanished into the background. The girl loved her stepbrother, couldn't stand to see him in pain any more than Jasmine could.

"I don't know, love. I'm sorry, but I don't."

Ellie and Lenore looked on in worry, and Jasmine turned away from them.

"Come on," Zoe said, still kneeling with him on the blanket. Cradling him. "Let's talk about this."

Kev sagged down into himself even further. "Talk about what? Pippa's gone. She walked around the tree three times and vanished. It's like she was tempting fucking fate, daring the tree, and it dared, and now she's gone!"

"What tree's this?" Zoe asked.

"Big tree up on the hill. Growing out of a shrine. Or a slab. The Wednesday Tree, they call it." He stood again, shrugging Zoe's hand from his shoulder. He looked around at all of them, eyes red, face slack. "Please, don't wind me up. This isn't a joke. She hasn't just . . . run off. She's gone!"

Nathaniel had been sitting on his own blanket, taking it all in like a bystander at a family quarrel, yearning for an exit. But this was no quarrel, and Nathaniel wasn't like that at all. He was a friend to the whole family, caring about all four.

"I'm sorry, mate," Nathaniel ventured, trying to catch Kev's gaze. "None of us knows this Pippa. Is she someone new?"

Nathaniel hadn't moved any closer, sticking to his own blanket, but suddenly it felt to Jasmine like they were all standing too close, crowding Kev. She watched the distress on his face. *He looks . . . Fuck, he looks wired.*

"Kev—" she said, but then Ellie stepped forward and grabbed his attention. Drew his focus.

It was always Ellie, and in that moment Jasmine felt a rush of respect and love for her daughter. So young, and yet so wise.

"Hey, bro, let's talk this through," Ellie said. She didn't reach out for him, but her voice seemed to calm him a little. He was much taller than she, and over the past year or two he'd grown broad and strong as the man emerged from the boy. But right then, Ellie was the center around which they all orbited.

Kev looked at his sister with pleading eyes.

"Ellie, you believe me, don't you? Pippa wouldn't just do this for fun, not after she heard me shouting for her. And I was really shouting for a while, I searched and searched, she wouldn't have done it! She was teasing me, you know, and we were gonna . . . She just went. Vanished. Gone."

"Okay, Pippa's gone," Ellie said, as if she had the first clue who Pippa might be. "So maybe we need to sit and think about where she could be, and what happened, and then we can decide what to do."

Kev froze. He blinked a few times at Ellie, and Jasmine almost asked him then. He'd traveled here before them, and he'd had time to circulate around the festival. It was a family event, but there were always drugs at these things. He didn't seem drunk, and she'd been close enough to know he didn't smell of booze. But he did seem different. His focus was somewhere else, somewhere different.

"You don't believe me," he said to Ellie.

Her pause in answering, her indrawn breath as she thought about what to say, was enough.

"Fuck!" he shouted.

Jasmine looked around. He was drawing attention from other festival goers, a few nervous glances their way.

"Kev," she said, "try to keep it down."

"Fuck!" he said, much louder this time.

"Kev, calm the hell down!" Jasmine stepped forward, standing just behind Zoe, feeling protective of her wife and their whole family. She hated conflict or arguments, a hangover from a difficult childhood. Her own brother was a drunk and constantly in and out of police custody, and she'd grown into an adult who avoided confrontation as much as she possibly could. Often she viewed that as a weakness, and if she and her wife argued it was usually Zoe who had the last word. But sometimes to defuse a situation you had to take control of it, and guide it down.

"How can you tell me to be calm when Pippa's—"

"Have you taken something?" Jasmine asked.

The scene froze. Jasmine, Zoe, Kev, Ellie, Lenore, and Nathaniel became a motionless tableau amongst the energetic and buzzing social dance of the festival. Music still boomed in the background, and the constant chatter of fellow fans, and all the other exotic smells and sounds. But for that moment their own extended family existed in its own small bubble.

Kev stared at her, and in his eyes she saw something that gave her pause. He was truly, genuinely afraid. "No, 'Mum'," Kev said. And the way he said Mum drove a dagger into her heart.

"So you met someone," Ellie said, trying to calm the moment, save the day. "She teased you then ran off, but—"

Kev left. It was so quick, so sudden, that they all merely stood there and watched him sprinting away through the crowd. He nudged one man's arm and spilled beer, jumped over another small group's blanket, and in moments he was lost to the crowd, running across the front of the main stage area and towards the large central hub of the festival site, where dozens of produce pavilions were set around the ancient stone circle at its centre.

"Kev!" Ellie called after him, but way too late.

"Shit," Jasmine said.

"Not your fault," Zoe said.

"Yeah, but—"

"Not your fault, Mum," Ellie echoed. "Not at all."

"What the hell's up with him?" Jasmine asked. "Zoe?"

"Maybe drugs, like you said," Zoe admitted. "But I hope the hell not." She looked shattered with worry, even disoriented.

"I don't think he's taken anything," Ellie said. "I'd know."

"Zoe, come on," Jasmine said, touching her face, making sure Zoe focused on her. "He won't have gone far. We'll find him and sort it out."

Whatever was happening to Kev—some weird episode, a girl treating him badly, or even if he had taken something he shouldn't have—Jasmine couldn't get the way he'd called her *Mum* out of her mind. She and Zoe considered each other's children their own. It was a precious feeling, an extension of their love, an expression of belonging together. She hated the idea that Kev might think otherwise.

They turned to go after Kev, hand in hand, when someone called Jasmine's name. She looked round and froze at the sight of Frank Turner's tour manager. She'd spoken to him earlier, and she knew why he was here. She felt herself being torn in half.

"Jasmine Swift?" the guy said, studying her. He must have seen a thousand faces in the past couple of hours, so she didn't take offense.

"That's right," she said.

The man weaved through a few groups and around blankets on the grass. He caught sight of Ellie and smiled. "You need to come now," he said. "We were expecting you at the backstage entrance fifteen minutes ago."

"Yeah, sorry, we've had a . . . thing going on."

The man shrugged. "Your girl's got a ten minute slot starting in fifteen minutes. That's all we've been able to pull with the festival organisers. And like I said before, this is pretty fucking unusual, to say the least."

He didn't seem irritated at having been asked to arrange this, more astonished that he'd pulled it off. But when the lot of them just stood about staring at one another, Jasmine noticed the way his brow furrowed. He'd already begun to regret having called in a favor on their behalf. She looked at Zoe, helpless. They ought to go after Kev, of course. Jasmine knew she ought to support her wife, help look out for their boy, but a flash of anger rippled through her.

Fucking Kev, again, she thought.

Hated herself for it.

None of them moved for several seconds. Too many seconds for the tour manager not to notice. He began to speak, backing up a step, raising his hand as if to wave off this moment, this chance of a lifetime. Jasmine panicked inside, wanted to scream.

Lenore saved her. Saved Ellie.

"I'll go after him," Lenore said. She and Ellie were standing close, holding hands. Lenore turned to her with a smile. "You go and *smash it*."

"No, no, I'll go," Nathaniel said, rising from his blanket. "I'll find him and get him to the medical tent, and you come and find us there afterwards."

"You're sure?" Jasmine asked, and she thought, *Shit I hope he's sure*, because this was Ellie's big moment. She knew how nervous her daughter was about it, and she saw a simmering anger at what she'd done. But what mother would have turned down such an opportunity for her kid? No mother, that's who. And Lenore was right, Ellie was going to smash it.

"Of course I'm sure," Nathaniel said. "You all need to see Ellie's big moment, right? All of you together, and I'll hear it wherever I am. And Lenore will be filming, right?"

"Actually the whole performance will be filmed and put out on the festival's YouTube channel," the manager said.

"I think I'm going to puke," Ellie muttered.

"Go," Nathaniel said. "Go get 'em."

Jasmine saw the anguish on Zoe's face, stepped close and lowered her voice to whisper in her ear. "Listen, babe. You do what you have to do. Ellie will understand."

Zoe exhaled, lips pressed thinly together. "No . . . that's not fair to Ellie. She's my daughter, too, and this is too big. If Nathaniel will find Kev and sort out what he's so panicked about—and if he's . . . on something—then he can wait half an hour for his mother. I'm not going to let him take this away from Ellie, or from us."

Ellie overheard. She looked sad a moment, but then Zoe squeezed Jasmine's hand and went to Ellie, put a hand behind her back and started motoring her toward the stage.

"Move it, kid," Zoe said.

"Oh, and Frank's said she can use his guitar," the manager said.

Ellie's eyes opened wide, and she glanced at Jasmine. Mother and daughter mouthed to each other, *Fucking hell!*

"See you later," Nathaniel said. As he left to find the troubled Kev, Jasmine and Zoe started following the manager towards the side of the main stage. She looked back and Ellie and Lenore were high-fiving, and Jasmine felt tears threatening.

"What a day," Zoe said.

"Yeah," Jasmine said, and she stole a quick kiss. "And it's only just begun."

CHAPTER 5 ◆ KEV

Kev knew his mums didn't believe him. If they had, there was no way they'd have let him run off on his own. He felt as if he might rip his skull open to make room for the thoughts swirling in his head. Two impossible things in one day—hadn't there been something in *Alice in Wonderland* about that?

Alice in Wonderland. Like Pippa, she'd vanished. Alice had been inspired by a thousand stories of people wandering into faerie, vanishing in the woods. Had Pippa fallen through the looking glass? Had she chased a rabbit down a fucking hole?

Kev rushed through the crowd, wishing Pippa was taller so he could spot her amongst them. Or wishing he could fly, because why not? If Pippa could just walk widdershins round a tree and just poof out of existence like some kind of magician's assistant vanishing from a box, surely he could spread his wings and fly over the heads of these laughing, singing, swaying, sweaty people—real and tangible people with blood and bones, people he could reach out and touch.

"Pippa!" he screamed, craning his neck, pushing roughly between two men. He cried her name again, then clutched the sides of his head. "Fuck!"

So stupid. No reason to think she'd just reappear here in the crowd. But maybe she hadn't really vanished. Maybe it had been a trick all along, she'd slipped away into the trees in the moment his view of her had been obscured by the Wednesday Tree. Which would mean she could be anywhere, maybe frantic that the trick had gone so wrong. Maybe she was looking for him right now, the same way he was looking for her.

Kev laughed to himself, gleeful at the thought.

Maybe a bit more loony than gleeful, because what about his mums? What about Ellie and Lenore? Even Nate and fucking Sally were too kind to go along with anything like this, and . . .

They'd never heard of Pippa before in their lives. Didn't know who he was talking about. Initially he'd told himself they were taking the piss, but his mum and Jasmine loved him, and Ellie adored him, and they'd never do such a thing. And their eyes—he'd seen the truth in their eyes, in the way they worried for him. Worried he'd lost his mind.

Worried he'd started using again.

Fucking Jasmine, he thought in rage.

But the real pain in his heart was that he couldn't blame her. What else were any of them supposed to think? Kev wished he was high—had never wished so hard to be flying. Then maybe some of this would make sense, or at least it wouldn't need to.

Pippa. Oh, Christ . . . what the fuck?

Kev shoved through another cluster of punters and found himself facing a line of concession booths. Beer, chips, quick curries, long lines. Kev glanced left and right, lost now, no idea where to go or what the point had been of storming off. He needed help to find Pippa, needed security or police, needed someone on the stage to ask every person in the crowd to look for Pippa.

He turned, thinking he might rush the stage, and saw Nathaniel muscling through a circle of people moshing half-heartedly and half-drunkenly to the intermission music now that Stormzy had gone off stage.

Nathaniel called his name.

The worry and kindness on his face nearly broke Kev, but then he remembered that nobody believe him and knew Nathaniel would be no help at all. He turned back toward the hills, looked between two of the concession booths and saw a path leading upward, a different Valhalla Hill trail, this one with a sign at the bottom and heavy foot traffic heading both up and down.

A big bastard with an overflowing beer in his fist bumped into Kev while walking from the concession, his head turned toward his mate. Beer spilled onto Kev's shirt and pants, slid down into his shoe, but even as his anger rose, his mind replayed the last thing the big bastard had said in the moment just before they'd collided.

" . . . said he just fuckin' disappeared, mate! You believe that? Like, walked into the midst of the stone fuckin' circle and blinked out like he was erased, summat straight outta Doctor Fucking Who—"

Collision. Warm beer spilling down Kev's leg. Inside his shoe.

He stared at the big bastard, who knitted his brows with the perfect blend of challenge and dismissal. "Oi, watch where you're going, ya—"

Kev grabbed his wrist. More beer spilled over the rim of the cup. "Who disappeared? You just said someone vanished. Where did this happen?"

The bastard twisted Kev's hand away, breaking his hold, but looked at him with wariness instead of hostility, maybe thinking Kev some kind of nutter. *And probably not wrong.*

"It's nothing, mate," the big bastard said, gesturing toward the path beyond the concession booths with his sloshing beer. "Just saw a couple of girls losing their minds, dragging one of the security guards up the hill cuz they claim some bloke went into the stone circle and turned fucking invisible or vanished, like."

Kev took two steps toward the gap between the concession booths, staring at the foot traffic on the path that led to the stone circle. Couldn't be a coincidence, could it? Not a chance.

"I figure them girls is on something, right? Or havin' a laugh," the big bastard went on.

Kev wasn't listening anymore.

Nathaniel caught up to him then, breathless, wheezing, laughing at himself as he tried to catch his breath.

"Hey, don't run off again," he said, resting one hand on Kev's shoulder. "Give us a second and we'll search for this Pippa together."

It was "this" that made him flinch, reminded him his family had no idea who he was searching for. The girl he loved. The girl he hoped to marry. Maybe it wasn't their fault. Maybe Pippa hadn't vanished at all, but been erased, like the big bastard had said.

Kev looked at sweaty, huffing Nathaniel. "Thanks. Really. But I can't wait for you."

He took off between the concessions, storming toward the busy trail, headed for the stone circle and whatever answers it held.

CHAPTER 6 ◆ ELLIE

Ellie let her mum take her by the hand as they snaked through the crowd, making for the stage as fast as the throng would allow. Any other day she'd have balked at letting her mum drag her around like she was still a toddler, but she barely felt the tug of her mother's hand. Something carried her toward the stage as if a wave had lifted her, building, ready to crash her onto the shore. Her heart felt full, thrumming. Her throat went dry.

The tour manager—what the hell had his name been?—led them around the side of the stage, flashing a plastic badge at the security guards. Only when one of the guards took her own plastic badge, glanced at it, and let it fall again before waving her through, did Ellie even remember the tour manager putting the lanyard around her neck. Her mom had one, too.

"Jasmine, Ellie, let's move!" the tour manager said.

You should remember his name, Ellie thought. *He made this happen just as much as Frank did. Ah, hell, you're a complete shit.*

Yet even as that regret took root, Ellie couldn't focus on it. The tour manager quickened his pace to a trot once they were through security. Other festival staff and musicians were around, some working and some chatting. Holy fuck, was that Laura Jane Grace? Was she even on the bill, or was she going to make a surprise appearance?

Ellie's head was on a swivel, taking it all in, a huge grin on her face.

"Still hate me?" her mum asked.

Ellie didn't hate her, but the question brought all the anxiety back in a torrent. She faltered a bit, fell a couple of steps behind, not sure she could really do this, even if everyone else had faith she'd smash it.

"Let's move!" the tour manager snapped.

Ellie looked past her mum and saw the stairs at the side of the stage. Equipment and scaffolding had been built up as if to construct a fortress, but those stairs were the way in, and the plastic badge dangling from her lanyard gave her access.

A chill prickled at the back of her neck and she felt that *something* wash over her again. It drove her forward, stole her breath away. Ellie nearly forgot her mum was beside her and when she reached the steps she ran up after the tour manager like she'd always belonged on that stage.

In the off-stage area, the wings, crew members rushed around, moving equipment, tuning instruments. A massive, bearded man hurried by, barking into a headset, and she spotted two men talking together in the shadow of a stack of amplifiers. What drew her eyes to them was the utter calm they projected. While everyone else rushed around as if averting a crisis, these two seemed not to have a care in the world. Ellie recognized Stormzy, of course. He'd just wrapped his set and up close he was just as fit and gorgeous as in the videos she'd seen, but she barely gave him a glance because the other guy was both one of her favorite songwriters and her benefactor for the day.

Tall and skinny, tattooed arms bared in his *Guise on Tour* t-shirt, Frank turned and saw them coming. He patted Stormzy on the arm and made a beeline for Ellie, as if he'd expected her—and of course he had, but she'd never really believed it until this moment. As he strode toward them, beard neatly trimmed but hair unruly, smiling like he was having the time of his life, he raised a hand to a crew member and shouted something, but Ellie's internal buzz drowned out the words.

The tour manager—she no longer cared that she couldn't recall his name—introduced Ellie and her mum, and Ellie blinked in surprise because for a few moments she'd forgotten her mum was even with her.

"Jasmine," Frank said to her mum, reaching out a hand. "Thanks for dragging her up here. You've got a talented girl."

Mum beamed. Thanked him.

The roadie came over, handed Frank his guitar. Frank slipped the strap round his own shoulder and strummed it, plucked a few chords, found a string out of tune and adjusted it, then slipped the guitar off and held it out for her to take.

"Fuck's sake," she breathed.

Frank laughed. Not at her. Or, not exactly. He helped her slip the guitar strap over her head and then autopilot kicked in, and Ellie adjusted the length of the strap to put it at the right height for her—Frank was fucking tall. She'd always wondered if he looked so tall because he was so skinny, but no, he was tall.

"Hey. Ellie." He put a hand on her arm, steadied her, eyes fixed on hers. "You're gonna be brilliant. Trust me. What'll you play?"

She went blank a moment, eye to eye with him. In that quiet moment, that something returned and she felt the lure of the stage as if someone had set a hook in the middle of her chest and begun to reel her in. Her body yearned to be there and she had to fight to keep her feet from moving before she'd even answered.

Ellie heard her mum sigh, knew Jasmine was about to answer for her, and no fucking way would she let that happen. She might only be seventeen, might have gotten up here by the grace of mum and Frank and tour-manager-guy, but for Lenore and for the band and yeah, fuck yeah, for her own bloody self, she was going to play what her gut demanded.

Sort of.

"You liked that cover of 'Creep' I did," Ellie said. "I guess I've got time for two songs, so I'll do that first to get them on my side, and then I'll risk an original, this one I wrote called 'Girl and Guitar.'"

Frank gave a slow nod of satisfaction. "That'll be perfect. The punters'll love it."

What the hell? Yeah, they'd played "Girl and Guitar" at the party Frank had seen the video of, but he remembered it? Ellie wondered if she might be dreaming all of this? She'd written a lot of songs, but "Girl and Guitar" might be her most personal, and also the one that had made things more pleasantly awkward between her and Lenore than ever, given that the chorus identified her sexuality as "any pretty, sweaty girl with a growl in her voice and a guitar in her hands." It didn't mean Ellie had zero interest in guys—she'd never opened herself up like that to anyone—but the song put into words the one thing she found irresistible.

"Come on," Frank said, and she didn't have to be asked twice. Her feet were already in motion, that hook in her chest reeling her toward center stage even faster than Frank could escort her.

"You too, Mum," Frank called over his shoulder.

Ellie nodded to herself as she walked toward the microphone at center stage. It was right that her mum should be there. Frank went to the mic first. Recognizable as he was, the crowd roared a greeting for him, maybe thinking he was going to do a song with her playing. But then he went into an introduction, commanding the crowd to give Ellie's mum a round of applause.

Someone right down the front screamed "I love you, Jasmine," and Ellie scanned faces and found that somehow Lenore and Zoe had found their way to within forty feet of the stage.

Lenore beamed at her. Ellie's heart lifted.

That something tugged at the hook in her chest and she forgot all about Lenore. And Zoe. And Mum. And Frank Turner.

Introductions were complete. Frank put a hand at the small of Jasmine's back and hustled her into the wings of the stage. The fingers of Ellie's left hand contorted to find the first chord for the Tori Amos version of "Creep."

Strangers cheered for her.

She played the first few chords. "When you were here before, couldn't look you in the eye . . . "

Her hands faltered. Her lips exhaled a hiss into the microphone, as if the song she'd intended to sing had been expelled from her body, and something else had taken its place.

Again, Ellie began to sing. Only now the song wasn't hers at all. She drew a breath into her lungs that seemed to fill her up completely. A shudder close to ecstasy made her tremble, a joyful smile on her face.

The voice that came from her lips felt as if it were not her own. Beautiful, ethereal . . . ancient . . . the song emerged from within her, filling every amplifier, every speaker, every ear. Ellie had never felt anything like this before. *This is music,* she thought. *This is joy. This is magic.*

Inside that magic, she felt the stirring of malice, and as that malice spread through her, Ellie began to dance. Slow and languorous, arms weaving in the air, hips swaying, she felt the song, the dance, the malice flow out of her, and she heard her own ancient voice as it filled the air, filled the fields and the hills around them.

Just out of the corner of her eye, Ellie spotted her mother begin to jerk and flail offstage in a kind of obscene pantomime of the dance Ellie herself had begun. Beside Jasmine, a bearded stage hand jerked backward, arms outflung, spine bent, twisting himself into the same hideous dance.

It spread to Frank next.

One after another, the people began that horrid dance.

Ellie tried to stop singing. Tried to stop dancing, to step away from the microphone, but her body was no longer her own.

She wept as she sang.

The ancient song went on and on.

CHAPTER 7 ◆ JOSHUA

Joshua wasn't deluded enough to believe that anyone might recognize him. He had a bit of an underground following, and his steady output of independent albums provided an intermittent income. He sold most of them at the gigs he performed across the country, at local pub events, village fetes, folk festivals, and sometimes even hired to play weddings or, in one memorable gig, a funeral. He also had a website from which he sold CDs and other merch — t-shirts, mugs, pens, the usual stuff, as well as two volumes of his attempts at poetry— but the site needed upgrading, and there was a disconnect between his fingers and any form of technology more complex than a guitar amp.

His music was his life, and he'd settled into the idea that he was never really going to make it big.

Now, the Valhalla Festival gig. The Ragnar Stage, true, but even there he'd likely have a thousand people watching and listening to his music. He'd shipped a couple of boxes of CDs to the festival to sell after his slot, and now he was close, so close, and what should have been one of the most exciting moments of his life felt . . .

Strange.

"Weird," he said. "Just fucking weird."

Joshua felt watched. It reminded him of a bad trip he'd had in his twenties after eating mushrooms, a paranoid episode that had lasted for three days and had him hiding in a cupboard, sheltering beneath a staircase, and in the narrow cob-webbed attic of the old Victorian house where he'd been renting a room, all in an effort to escape whoever or whatever was watching him. This wasn't as bad, and with the sensation settling amidst crowds of people it was highly likely he *was* being watched.

Not as bad, but different. He felt observed. Tracked. Followed.

Hurrying through the milling crown towards the Ragnar Stage, he glanced behind him several times. He was still sweating from climbing up and over Valhalla Hill, and the encounter with the troubled kid played on his mind. But the more time he spent in the embrace of the festival, the better he began to feel. The smells and sounds, the sights and tastes of cooking food on the air, all brought him home. And the guitar case on his back obviously marked him, because one time when he glanced to his right he realised that he *was* being watched.

She was tall, beautiful, long braided hair falling across her shoulders, short skirt emphasising shapely legs, armless red shirt unbuttoned just one or two buttons too low for decorum's sake. But fuck it, this was a festival.

Not her.

Joshua paused. The woman stood motionless in the flow of people moving all around her, some carrying food or drink, others heading from one stage to another in this brief pause in music. He saw that quite a few of the people were headed towards the Ragnar Stage, and the familiar teeth of impostor syndrome gnawed at his soul.

She was looking right at him.

"Joshua Standen?" she asked as she came closer.

"Yeah."

Not her, he thought. *Whoever's watching me . . . it's not her.*

"Oh fuck, I came here to see you, but I didn't think I'd *see* you, you know?"

"Gotta get to the stage somehow," he said. He was trying to be cool, but she was hypnotic, and now that he saw her nervousness and her voice shook when she spoke, the imposter syndrome bit in deeper than ever before.

I'm on stage in ten minutes. Can it, Joshua. Control it. Chill.

"I love your stuff, you music's just great, how come you're not backstage, have you been running, do you want me to help you with—"

"Carry this if you like," he said, and he slipped the guitar case from his shoulders. It had started hurting his arms, and he needed to be loose and comfortable once he hit the stage. "But yeah, I'm in a rush, traffic problems and I've walked a couple of miles to get here on time."

The woman seemed speechless. She held his guitar case in both hands, holding it across the front of her body instead of slinging it over her shoulders. Joshua started for the stage, and the woman walked close beside him.

"So what's your name?"

"Jemima."

He glanced at her.

"My parents are hippies."

"Nothing wrong with hippies," Joshua said.

"Yeah, well."

He saw her watching him, but it wasn't her, the eyes he felt on him were more analytical, more . . . cutting. Her gaze held no real weight. Her attention was open and honest. The scrutiny he felt from somewhere else was more secret. More dark.

"First time at the festival?" he asked.

"Yeah, first time here. I got into your music only last year, the 'Moment's End' album, really helped me through a rough time. And when I saw you were playing here I persuaded two of my girlfriends we had to come and see you. And the rest of the festival, of course."

"Sure," he said. "Some great acts here this year." It felt good, hearing that she'd come to see him above all the other amazing bands. Eat that, Stormzy! Hell, it wasn't something he heard every day. Not even once a year.

"So after your gig, can we get a drink?" she asked.

"Only if you let me take you to Ragnarok."

"Is that a euphemism?"

He glanced at her again. She was smiling. *Holy shit*, Joshua thought, *be cool, man. Be cool.*

"It's a private bar for the bands and their guests," he said. "But yeah, it's also the Viking heaven, I guess."

Be cool. Be cool.

"Sounds great. I can't wait. So much Viking stuff, where'd all that come from?" Jemima asked.

They were approaching the stage, and Joshua headed for the hoardings and the gate to the right of the stage. Security were there, and he dug in his pockets for his pass. *Five minutes*, he thought. He needed a piss, a drink, and a glance over his set list one more time. His nerves were frayed.

And something at Valhalla felt very different. The festival was buzzing, but beneath it all was a calm intelligence watching, observing, and holding its breath. Or maybe he'd just inhaled some tainted pot on his way through the throng.

"This was the site of a massacre," he said. "A thousand years ago this year, the villagers who lived hereabouts lured in a band of Viking invaders and hacked them to death."

"Oh, lovely," Jemima said. "And this festival's a celebration?"

"Commemoration," he said. "There's so much more to it, so much history, and the place is fascinating. It's . . . a draw. I come every year, even every third year when there's no festival and the site's left fallow."

"Maybe I'll come, too," she said.

"Maybe." He smiled, and among the chatter and movement and colours and chaos, they shared a loaded moment. *This hardly ever happens to me*, Joshua thought, but though it made him feel good, it didn't drive away the unsettled feeling that had enveloped him since coming down from Valhalla Hill. "I'll tell you all about it afterwards."

"In Ragnarok," she said, and as she handed him his guitar case she performed a delicious dance of excitement, and Joshua shamed himself by looking where he really shouldn't.

"I've got to go. Hope you and your friends enjoy the show."

"Oh, I've got to go and meet them! They won't believe me when I tell them I met you, they really won't." She actually looked worried.

"What's your favourite song of mine?"

"Oh, *Heart of Chords*, first and last and always."

"I'll dedicate it to you. Your girlfriends will believe you then."

"Thank you, Joshua," she said. "I mean it." She looked suddenly serious, and he saw something in her eyes, a dark shimmer, then a glint like light glimmering from a polished blade. Then she turned and was gone, and he spent a few seconds watching her as she pushed her way into the crowd.

The crowd that was gathered in front of the Ragnar Stage, ready to watch him.

"Fuck me, what a day," he muttered.

He passed through the security gate into the backstage area, where a runner found him and guided him up into the rear of the Ragnar Stage. Yes he was late, no he hadn't tuned his guitar, yes he could go on five minutes late but he'd still have to come off at the same time. And Joshua was fine with that. He took that extra five minutes to ground himself, take a drink and a leak, tune his guitar, and find a level of peace and calm.

Even alone with no one around him, he felt watched.

"You're up," the runner said. "Break a leg, man."

"Cheers."

Joshua waited in the wings while he was introduced, and then he walked out into the sunlight. The crowd cheered, and he heard a high, long shriek that he hoped was Jemima. His heart was hammering, he was still sweating, but the guitar was melded to his hands, as much a part of him as his limbs, his heart.

"Thank you Valhalla!" he said. "Is everyone having a good festival?"

A loud cheer.

"This really is the best of them."

Another cheer.

"Okay, so let's get this show on the road. This one's for my new friend Jemima, it's called *Heart of Chords*." As he strummed the first chord he spotted Jemima in the crowd, and she gave him a soft smile. This was going to be a very good day.

CHAPTER 8 ◆ KEV

Something scratched at Kev's brain, like a finger working at the inside of his skull, picking, scraping. He caught sight of Nathaniel rushing up the hill towards him and at first he thought Nathaniel's frown was from exertion. The hill was short but steep, and Kev's own heart was hammering as if to remind him, *Slow down, slow the fuck down!* He was younger and fitter than Nathaniel. He was—

What was that sound, that feeling in his head? Like nails on bone, but also backed by something beautiful, compelling. Something that made him want to . . . just . . .

Kev jerked around, facing away from Nathaniel, and his limbs felt suddenly loose and fluid as he began to sway where he stood. He was dancing to a music he couldn't quite hear, but which sang inside his skull. He caught a whisper of something on the air. And then he set eyes on the stone circle, and what was happening around it, and his awkward movements stopped cold.

There were thirteen stones, each taller than the tallest person, and wider than the widest. They were stuck solid in the ground, and the circle gave the impression of having been there for thousands of years, though many stone circles around the south-west had been placed much more recently as false monuments or tourist lures. Whatever the truth, the effort to haul these giant rocks to the top of this short, steep hill must

have been immense. A temple, an astronomical map, an ancient place of worship or fledgling science—whatever its purpose had once been was lost now, swallowed within what it had become. A place of chaos. A place of fear, and grief.

People were huddled around the outside of the stone circle in pairs or small groups, and many of them were upset. They cried or rocked where they sat, hugging each other or existing in a lonely form of grief or shock. One woman wearing a bowler hat tapped at one of the stones with a black walking stick, the insistent *tack, tack* sound keeping time with the weird song inside his head. An older woman reached out for the stones, two people holding her back, the three of them frozen in a motionless tableau filled with stress and coiled energies. A small child, seemingly on his own, walked back and forth between two standing stones, holding out his left hand and right hand alternately as if to skim an invisible wall between the stones. And were his fingertips causing a stir in the air? Were his fingers shorter than they should have been? Did they leave trails of blood on the air that misted away to a pink haze?

Every strange thing happening around the perimeter of the stone circle seemed linked to something within. Yet there was no sign of anyone inside— no movement, no life. It was empty apart from a large flat central slab. Kev couldn't shake the idea that it was an altar, and he also couldn't blink away the idea that it glimmered with spilled blood, its calm surface reflecting a clear blue sky speckled with clouds that were absent when he looked up. *A sky from somewhere else*, he thought, and he wondered why no one was inside the circle, and he remembered what the big bastard had said.

"Kev, come with me, there's something . . . " Nathaniel began, and grabbed his arm. But he wasn't looking at Kev. He was staring into the circle.

"That's odd," Nathaniel said.

"What's odd?" Kev asked. *Everything*, he thought. *Everything since the moment Pippa walked around the Wednesday Tree has been odd, and now maybe this is the place where I'll find her.*

"—just vanished—"

"Jamie! Jamie!"

"—got to go myself, got to, but I'm scared, I want her back but I saw her here and then gone and—"

"Oh, God. Oh, God."

"—something to do with the festival, an optical illusion with mirrors, and there'll be a bar inside or an orgy or something."

"Security! *Security!*"

"Oh, God. Oh, God."

"—and what the fuck is that music? Can you hear that? Can you hear that . . . *scraping?* That *itching?*"

Kev caught snatches of conversation from all around the empty stone circle, but he realized the last sentence was from Nathaniel.

"What's odd?" he asked again.

Nathaniel shook his head, then turned and held Kev's shoulders. They locked eyes but Nathaniel seemed to see through him to somewhere further away. "Come with me . . . Medical tent . . . Something's . . . " He frowned and shook his head again, harder this time, as is trying to shake a fly from his ear. "Something in the air."

Nathaniel looked around at the other people experiencing their own upsets, and Kev could see the disapproval in his eyes, the judgement.

It wasn't drugs. Kev knew what drugs felt like. Booze, too. This was different.

"Pippa might be in there," he said, and once voiced the idea seemed clear and solid, as if it was something he'd been trying to grab onto for a while. Now he would not let it go. He looked into the empty stone circle and the emptiness bore a weight and depth. As he shrugged Nathaniel's hands from his arms, the taller man sighed heavily and walked directly towards the space between two standing stones. He stepped over a man sprawled on the ground, edged past a couple who were hugging and crying together.

"Nathaniel?" Kev said.

Something in the air, he thought, and perhaps Nathaniel was right. But it wasn't the smell of illicit drugs. The strange sound he heard was a song, and people heard a song in countless different ways.

"Wait," Kev said.

Nathaniel paused at the edge of the circle and glanced back. "Once you know Pippa isn't here, whoever she is, we're all leaving this place."

Everyone else had fallen silent, watching Nathaniel.

"Don't," someone said, or maybe it was a mass of voices combined as one.

Nathaniel stepped forward and something seemed to solidify in the air, in Kev's mind, and he heard the strains of music and the ululating voice from behind him, back towards where the main stage thrust from the ground. It was a song both hypnotic and shattering, its words unknown yet translated by his subconscious into something malign. His blood betrayed him. His muscles unfroze and he started moving again, swaying, and everything that happened around him became another part of that music and song.

Nathaniel stepped in between two standing stones and disappeared. Between blinks he was there and then gone, and the music appeared to reach a subtle crescendo in celebration.

"Another one down," someone said from Kev's right, and he didn't even turn to see who had spoken. The words were swallowed by the hypnotic music and dispersed. He took another step forward, and rather than grief or fear he found himself reaching a level of clarity that he'd been seeking since the moment Pippa had walked behind that tree and not emerged from the other side.

I'm not mad, he thought. *They'll see that now. Everyone has seen that.*

His walk turned into a run, and as he passed through the perimeter of stones and into the circle they contained, he felt Pippa's name building from within.

"Pippa," he said, as the world outside disappeared and everything within the stone circle became his whole world.

That strange music vanished, replaced by wet sounds of dripping and settling meat. The hint of pot and cooking on the air was replaced by the tang of insides turned out.

The clearing outside the circle looked overgrown and forgotten, the gathered crowd nowhere in sight, as if they had never been there. Inside the circle, however, was far from empty. The flat stone slab at its centre was buried beneath a pile of torn, tattered bodies. They wore all styles and shades of clothing, but the overriding colour was red. Wounds gaped. Flesh was open. Blood flowed and dripped, and the ground all around the wide slab was dark with it.

Kev skidded to a stop on the wet ground, unable to breathe, desperate to take another breath, to call his love's name again.

Other bodies were scattered around, ripped and torn and contorted into violent sculptures, as if savage murder were an art.

Pippa? Kev said, but no sound came, and he only spoke her name in his head.

Close to the pile of corpses lay Nathaniel. Kev recognized him from the tee shirt he'd been wearing, and the knee-length shorts, and the fuzz of grey hair on the head that had been cleft in two, spilling brains across the grass.

Closer to Kev, just a few metres away, a woman was clawing at her midriff in an effort to haul her spilled insides back into her stomach. A shape appeared beside her, little more than a shadow, but the shadow reached out an arm that glinted with a trace of sharp-edged blade and Kev heard the unmistakeable sound of metal swishing through the air. The woman's

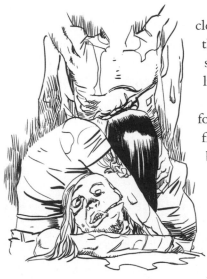

clenched mouth became a wide, red grin that reached around to the back of her skull. Her head fell back, and more of her life spilled out.

Kev blinked and looked away, searching for Pippa, hoping now that he would not find her. There must have been a hundred bodies there, maybe more, with the shadows of other things strolling between them. Vague, indistinct things, spectral killers that whispered and flickered and drew blood.

Across the other side of the circle another young woman suddenly manifested, walking in from outside. She caught Kev's eye, then looked around at the carnage.

Someone else looking for someone else, Kev thought.

And then he saw Pippa. She was close to the central slab, much of her body buried beneath others, but her face was tilted his way. She was dead. No one could look like that and be not dead.

Oh no Pippa, Pippa oh no, Kev tried to say.

The woman across the circle from him was jerked to one side by a fleeting shadow and her body fell open from stomach to neck, opening as if unzipped, emptying to the ground as the rest of her slumped and followed it down.

"Pippa," Kev managed aloud at last. He reached for his love, and something changed close to him, the air shimmering, a shadow appearing between him and her and blurring his vision and memory.

In the shadow, a bearded face.

He heard the swish of metal slicing air. And then he heard no more.

CHAPTER 9 ✦ ELLIE

She has never played this song, but she's known it her whole life.

Her mother's dance has settled into something calmer and more fluid, and Ellie senses that they are moving to the same tune, shifting the same way, almost filling the same space. Elsewhere around them, that is not the case. The bearded stage hand has danced himself into a knot, limbs protruding at odd angles, broken bones pressing against his skin from the inside. In a couple of places they have burst through in scarlet smiles. Others in the wings are twisting and turning themselves into similar contortions, some of them crying out in pain, others grunting in what might be agony or ecstasy.

Ellie can't understand how such beautiful music can bestow so much pain. She feels only joy and pleasure, and a calmness the likes of which she hasn't experienced for as long as she can remember. Her mother, too, is dancing to the joyous tones and beats. And yet spreading out from them—spreading out from *her*, because Ellie realizes she is the locus of this wonder- ful song—are ripples of pain. People jerk and jive into unnatural knots. Bones snap, providing a crin- kling backdrop to the music. Skin tears, flesh rips, a soft wet accompaniment.

Ellie closes her eyes to fully appreciate the sensuous tones thrumming through her body, from within and without. Behind those closed eyes she sees the shapes all around her, ambiguous fleeting shadows that grow more solid with each beat. They do not dance. But they do flow.

Being the voice of this song is everything she's meant to be and do. She was born for this, even before she was born.

Ellie opens her eyes and the new world she sees, this new world she is creating, is mostly red.

CHAPTER 10 ◆ LENORE

This isn't the song Ellie should be singing, Lenore thought again, and perhaps it was that foreknowledge that gave her the edge, the briefest flicker in time that allowed her to see and recognize that not only was this not the right song, but it was a very *wrong* song.

The way Ellie danced—that was also wrong, so much more confident and sensuous than her usual, awkward pose on stage. The audience always forgave her gawkiness due to the beauty of her voice and the way her fingers fluttered across her guitar, but this wasn't her. This wasn't the Ellie she knew, and probably loved.

In the same instant, the blink of her eyes, Lenore saw Jasmine's brief fit before she contorted herself to the music. She saw others dancing, on the wings of the stage at first, and then down at the front of the crowd, where people leaning against the metal barriers twisted and turned and flipped, necks creaking, backs bending the wrong way.

The wave of movement flowed out towards Lenore and Zoe, closer, closer, and the sounds of bones breaking and the grunts and screams of those dancing themselves into strange shapes added a backbeat of pain to the song flowing from the speakers.

Oozing, Lenore thought, and that seemed like the right way to describe the way the music spread through the crowd. As if it was moving out across the audience, a wave of something more solid, and tactile, and filled with dread. Like blood itself.

"Run," she said, grabbing Zoe's arm. But Zoe was entranced, swaying on the spot as the slow wave of twitchy dancing drifted out towards them.

"It's beautiful," Zoe said. "Look at her. Just look at our girl."

"That's not Ellie's song!" she shouted.

"No," Zoe said, "it's a cover, she's—"

"Zoe!" Lenore screamed, digging her fingers into the woman's arm so tightly that she felt bone beneath her fingertips. Zoe's dance slowed, but did not stop. She hardly felt the pain.

"But this is Ellie's big moment."

"They've found Kev," Lenore said, thinking on the spot. "They need our help. Kev needs you." Zoe's dreamy smile slipped just a little at the mention of her son, and Lenore tugged her along as she started running. Zoe stumbled after her, becoming more aware and alert with every step she took away from the stage.

Lenore let go of her arm and concentrated on running. She dodged through the crowd, most of whom were staring enrapt at the performance on the stage, and even then Lenore felt a twinge of something that might have been envy. *I could have been up there as well,* she thought, but she did not know this song. This was all Ellie, and it was a part of Ellie she didn't think she ever wanted to know.

What the fuck is happening?

She ran faster, because she could feel the music growing stronger around her, thicker, as if the air was taking on substance.

What the actual fuck?

To her left, something flitted across a gap between gyrating bodies. She glanced that way and saw nothing.

"Come on!" she shouted, because she wanted Zoe with her, she didn't want to be on her own.

To her right, at the corner of her eye, something shimmered like heat haze, an image forming out of nothing and taking the shape of a tall, thin man.

"Zoe, we've got to —" She glanced back and skidded to a halt, because Zoe had stopped twenty paces behind her and was dancing again, face turned to the sky, smiling as she moved, every part of her involved in the dance.

The air behind Zoe shimmered like a splash in thick water, then took on form. The hint of a figure, the mere suggestion of another tall, thin man, spectral tattoos on his face and throat. His head turned and his piercing eyes locked on Lenore, and a gap-toothed smile held her fast as something else moved quickly through the air, a horizontal flash. A ghostly blade, barely visible, the mere suggestion of what could only be a war axe.

The nigh-invisible blade met Zoe just above her hips. Her face went blank, her eyes wet with sorrow as her torso tipped forward and she folded

almost in two. Blood misted the air, and then flowed, and Lenore opened her mouth and screamed.

Something drove her on. She turned from the sickening image of Zoe cut almost in two, and the shape behind her that took more form when it was spattered with blood. She started running again, screaming again, and she was not the only one running and screaming. Others had seen what was happening, had seen the specters of dead men and women with Viking tattoos and translucent weapons, and were doing their best to escape the chaos, the death, and the terrible dance.

That she was not on her own gave her no comfort at all.

Lenore ran, and ran, while on the stage Ellie's hauntingly beautiful song continued. The voice of the friend she loved caught at her heart with cruel, barbed hooks, but she ran onward, through the dancing and murder, and the tempo of both picked up speed.

CHAPTER II ◆ JASMINE

Jasmine screamed inside herself but her throat would not give it voice. Instead when she opened her lips, only the song came out. The same song that her daughter sang, just a whisper, a rasp, an echo as if all her mouth could do was amplify the ancient melody that Ellie sang into life there on that stage. At that microphone.

As they danced.

Her body moved slowly at first but then faster, and faster still. Jasmine's head whipped around, her hair flying wild, muscles snapping in her neck. Her arms were wild, her knees jerking. Her left arm contorted behind her back with such ferocity that she felt a bone in her forearm snap and something tore inside her shoulder.

But the song swept through the crowd and Jasmine danced all the faster. Tears coursed down her face—tears of pain, but somehow, deeper inside her, an echoing that haunted her heart and head, also tears of pride. Watching her Ellie, her sweet girl, Jasmine felt something wake within her. Something new to her, but very, very old.

The thing inside her, the ancient woman now blinking awake in the sunlight of this new millennium, knew this song very well. It knew the dance and it knew the cruel vengeance the music carried. The ancient woman waking inside Jasmine had a name—Ulfhild. In the midst of the dance, the song singing in her bones, Jasmine knew what Ulfhild knew, that one thousand years before her people had been betrayed on this hill, seduced with empty promises of friendship and full tankards of ale, with music and with dance . . . and then murdered. Slaughtered, their blood soaking the land and the rocks, even as the music played on.

This, the last song the Vikings had ever sung in this place.

Ulfhild remembered. She remembered being grateful, as she died, that her son Trygve had been far afield, that he would live. And as the ancient woman inside her remembered Trygve, Jasmine felt the knell of recognition in her bones—those broken and those still whole. This had been her blood-line. Ulfhild to Trygve to Gudrun to Roar and on and on, until the blood descended to her—to Jasmine.

As she flailed about, dancing with such passion and violence that her left eye protruded from the socket and two of her vertebrae cracked, Jasmine felt pride rising again. Pride in her blood, in herself, and she raised her voice in song and twisted round to gaze again upon her daughter.

Ellie danced sinuously, unbroken, undying. She sang the last song of her people, finding the echo first of the night that Ulfhild had died, and then singing that thousand-year-old night alive again. Alive and full of murder.

Ellie was their descendant, too. She had their blood, and she had their song. With Ulfhild looking out through her eyes, Jasmine saw the music take hold, saw the brutal dance spread through the crowd in a slow, rolling wave. In ones and twos, and by the dozens, people danced and thrust and whipped themselves round till their bones broke and their brains turned to jelly in their skulls. Those who fell were stomped and trampled by the dance. The more fortunate among them were dead when they hit the ground and could not feel the shoes and boots that ground them into the dirt and smeared their blood until nothing but red mud lay beneath their feet.

The amplifiers carried the song, pushed the wave faster and further. A man fell from the scaffolding above the stage and crashed down onto a blanketed drum set on a riser. Broken, bleeding, he gyrated on top of the tarp and the drums and spilled onto the stage, half his face pulped by the fall, leaving a snail trail of viscera behind him. His shin bone had snapped and torn the skin. His left hand flapped uselessly atop his broken wrist.

Ulfhild leaned her head back and let the sweetness of the song of vengeance take flight from Jasmine's lips.

Still Ellie sang. Like an angel, her mother would have said.

Ulfhild breathed in with Jasmine's lungs, tasted the air for the first time in a thousand years. Death had been in the air that night, and here it was again. The scents of blood and fear filled her head, but beneath those she could taste the aroma of the earth and the woodlands, the damp ground, the trickle of a stream that ran down from the hill. The land the Vikings had claimed so long ago, and for which they had been murdered.

A smile touched Jasmine's lips—Ulfhild's smile—for out amongst the dancing, screaming, dying crowd she could see phantoms in the air. The lines blurred, mere suggestions of the proud warriors and shield maidens who had lived and died in this place, the mothers and fathers who had never been given the chance to raise their children here, whose futures had been extinguished at the point of a sword or the swing of an axe. They could never go back to that moment, never ignite any spark of life again, but when laughter rolled across the hill they called Valhalla, when the music began and the rhythm of the drums resonated with the stones, when the dead of this place understood that these fuckers were celebrating the anniversary of their murder, they woke.

Music woke them. Spite woke them. Vengeance woke them.

Now they breezed amongst the crowd wielding axes and daggers just as ephemeral as the warriors themselves. The lights caught the glint of an axe-edge or a ghostly eye, the stillness of a specter in the moment before a blade fell. They were barely there, but the blades still cut and cleaved and the blood still flowed. Hatred had a keen edge.

The ones in the crowd who were murdered were the fortunate ones. Those who danced themselves to death suffered far more. But each and every one understood death before it came for them, saw the carnage around them, and screamed for mercy. Trapped in the dance, in the song Ellie sang, they wailed in terror. As the dance continued to spread, those at the edges of the crowd tried to outrun its contagion. Ulfhild wondered if any of them would make it, wondered how fast they would have to be, how far they would have to run. She wondered how far the music of a thousand-year-old hatred would carry.

Far enough, she thought. Far enough.

With a final taste of the world, Ulfhild left Jasmine as swiftly as she had entered. The others of her village were bloodying their weapons and she wanted the same satisfaction. She craved to spill the blood of these singers and celebrants before they had all danced themselves to death.

Jasmine exhaled . . .

Continued dancing . . .

Tears streamed down her face as she watched the shimmer of the dead woman's soul as it drifted away from her. Her body already torn and broken by the dance, she yearned to collapse, wept with despair, and then leapt and spun and twisted her limbs at impossible angles. When she landed her right leg snapped. She fell to the stage, still jerking, thrashing. Her head struck the stage ever harder, thudding with the rhythm, until her skull cracked open. Even then she managed to jerk and twist and thrash a little bit more, until gray and red brain matter slid out onto the wood. The song released her at last.

CHAPTER 12 ◆ JOSHUA

Joshua lost himself in the song—his own song, an original he'd written while in one of his blackest periods, desperate to be in love, hollowed out by years of pouring more passion into his music than he ever seemed able to eke out of an audience. The fans who loved him really loved him, but there never seemed to be enough of them. He told himself any music-maker should consider themselves fortunate to have even a single stranger they could make scream out loud or jump around or laugh or cry just with the power of their music. Joshua had met a lot of those over the years. People whose hearts he'd touched with his voice and his guitar, people he'd made cry or laugh or embrace one another. People who'd shouted back to him, fist pumping, when he'd called to them from the stage. It was a bit of magic, every fucking time.

Today he had chills up his spine as he sang. The music thrummed in his bones like it hadn't done in months, maybe years. Just a handful of songs into his short set, Valhalla Festival felt like everything he'd dreamed it would be. Already he'd spotted Jay McAllister in the audience—Beans on Toast. The guy was a legend on the British folk scene and Joshua saw his head bobbing and a smile on his face and it fueled him, made him laugh out loud while he sang. Jay bloody McAllister. And he didn't want to make too much of it, but he'd caught a glimpse of green hair under a hoody and thought maybe, just maybe, he'd seen Billie Eilish and Finneas out there, in the smallish crowd gathered around the Third Stage. They were youngsters, really, and not the type of music he made, but lord he admired their sound, somehow both weighty and dreamlike at the same time.

All of that happened before the weird shiver, the thrum in his bones, the strange chord that seemed to strum within him. It threw him off and he frowned, lost half a verse of the song he was meant to be singing. He backed off the mic, played a little riff and got himself to the chorus so he could figure out which verse to slide into next. He could do the chorus on autopilot, and while he sang and played, he lent half an ear to that background noise, that thrum in the distance.

Joshua thought it came from the main stage. Distant music, a haunting melody, a lovely voice raised, though with his own guitar drowning it out he could only get the barest sense of it.

He glanced at his small audience again, looking for Jay McAllister, and found the man still there. McAllister wore a troubled expression, and for a heartbeat Joshua thought it was disappointment on his face. Shit. Fuck. Beans on Toast had seen him completely fumble the song and goddamn that was embarrassing.

Jemima stood just three faces to McAllister's right. Joshua had started out by playing his first song for her, hoping they'd get to know one another later, but when he saw the look on *her* face, he realized something more had distracted these people than just him fucking up his song.

He kept playing. He sang the last line of the chorus and let his fingers continue to roam across his guitar strings, kept the rhythm going. But more quietly, more sedately. As he quieted down, Joshua saw more faces in the crowd turn away and crane their necks to peer toward the main stage.

Finally, he heard the screaming.

His guitar pick slipped from his fingers. The note he played had nothing to do with the song he'd been in the middle of. Joshua's music stopped, but the screaming grew louder as more voices joined. Louder, and nearer.

On the small stage, Joshua held his breath and listened, staring out across the heads of the audience. Everyone around him had frozen, heads cocked, listening to the distant music and the screams, wondering what the hell was going on . . . and maybe also troubled by a tickle at the base of their skulls, just as he was. That little tickle that made him want to dance, in spite of the screaming.

He saw a ripple in the crowd. Bodies moving. Some people were running, fleeing as best they could, weaving amongst the audience and shoving people aside. Guitar banging against his hip, he stepped toward the edge of the stage and narrowed his eyes, trying to understand what he saw. A kind of wave moved toward him through the crowd, a slow rolling undulation

that seemed almost to pursue those who were trying to flee—the people who'd had the good sense to run away. That wave consisted of people dancing. So many had frozen, watching in confusion, listening to that song, but a few seconds after those in front of them began to dance, the next cluster of people followed suit.

And the way they danced . . . Joshua saw how wrong it was, how painful. A tall, slim, bald guy in a tank top threw his elbows back with such ferocity that broken bone burst through the skin round his clavicle.

Mind seared with that image, the sharp bone and torn skin and spatter of blood, Joshua whipped his head around in search of Jemima. He saw Beans on Toast start to run, but no sign of Jemima. Something shifted in his peripheral vision, a gauzy gray something like morning mist but alive and moving fast, and it paused behind a middle-aged dad who'd just grabbed hold of his teenage daughter to hustle her away from danger. For a fraction of an instant, that misty gray thing resolved itself and Joshua saw it—really saw it—and he thought he might be losing his mind. Towering, fearsome, iron rings knotted in his beard, the Viking could only be a ghost.

The ghost drove a sword of mist through the middle-aged dad's back, buried it to the hilt with such force that it stabbed the man's daughter, too. Just the tip of that blade, but it caught her in the hip. Punctured denim and flesh, probably knocked against the pelvic bone. The girl staggered backward, screamed at the sight of her father dying, and then the mist whipped away as if on a breeze and the ghost moved on. The girl caught her father's corpse as it fell. She knelt with him on the ground, but Joshua saw the wave of the dance approaching her and he knew what would happen next.

He sprang from the stage, guitar in hand. Beans on Toast nearly bowled him over and Joshua shoved him out of the way, intent on reaching the girl. In his mind's eye he imagined himself grabbing her by the wrist and yanking her away from her dead father, fleeing with her away from the impossible. They'd run for the exit, for the parking lots, as far and as fast as they could go. They'd run until they couldn't hear that eerie song coming from the main stage.

Joshua bounced off a security guard. The neck of his guitar caught the man in the side and Joshua spun around, nearly falling beneath the trampling feet of those who'd shaken themselves free of fascination to make a run for it. A stream of profanity spouting from his own lips, he ripped the guitar strap from around his neck and let the guitar fall to the ground. In the back of his mind he cringed as he thought of all the memories attached to that guitar, but what did that matter now?

A couple running in the opposite direction nearly clotheslined him with their linked hands. He spun again, and this time when he peered ahead, in the direction of the main stage, he had lost sight of the girl and her murdered dad.

Joshua glanced left and right, saw no sign of them, and then saw someone about half a dozen people ahead of him begin that jerking, twisting dance. The woman whipped her head back, leapt and spun, twisted her left leg at the knee, jerked violently in something more seizure than ballet. Joshua blinked as he realized it was Jemima, for whom he'd played a song, and with whom he'd imagined going home tonight.

Stunned and terrified, he backed up a step, then three more. They all began to dance like that, a whole swathe of the crowd ahead of him—so close, closer than he'd imagined that wave could have come so fast—and the girl, her dead father, and even Jemima vanished from his thoughts.

A man staggered to the left, tripped over his own feet, and went sprawling on the ground. A girl with blonde hair and dark eyeliner leaped over him to avoid falling—or maybe she'd been the one to shove him. She barreled forward, momentum carrying her on a collision course with Joshua. He caught her in his arms, held her up, locked eyes with her and saw fear and trauma to mirror his own.

She grabbed Joshua by the shirt. Buttons popped off as she yanked him into motion.

"Come on, ya daft prick!" she shouted.

Then Joshua was running, shoving past the mesmerized and the slow-on-the-uptake. Guitar forgotten, stage forgotten, Jemima forgotten, the girl and her dead dad forgotten, Valhalla forgotten. Only running mattered now. Outrunning the ghosts and the dance and the song that even now seemed to reach deep into the ancient part of his brain and call him back.

But he wasn't going back.

His eyes welled with terror and he clapped his hands over his ears and began to sing at the top of his lungs as he ran. Whatever black contagion that song held, whatever hideous power, he would never surrender to it.

He lifted his own voice in self-defense, sang as loud as he could—the first song that came into his mind. It was a double-time version of The Clash's "London Calling" and his heart and legs pumped in time with the beat.

Joshua sang louder. Ran faster.

Ahead of him, the girl began to sing along.

CHAPTER 13 ◆ LENORE

The man running behind Lenore was singing. Their voices combined to drown out the awful music still flowing across the festival site from Ellie on the main stage.

A bad, wrong song, Lenore thought. She had no idea how that could be coming from her friend, but she'd witnessed the effect it was having on the crowd. She had seen that flickering image appear, the tall horrible man cutting Zoe almost in half before her eyes.

Nothing made sense. Nothing but survival, and survival was running as far and as fast as she could. Many people were running in the same direction now, but there was no group effort here. This was pure panic. A man went down on her left and was trampled by those behind him. To her right, close to a burger stand, a woman was hanging onto the arm of a fallen child with both hands, pulling even as people tripped and ran over her son's battered body.

Lenore dodged a group of young men who were somehow still oblivious to the chaos. They were drunk, arms around each other's shoulders, singing and spinning in a slow circle. As she passed them by they split apart, a couple of them staggering back into her and sending her sprawling. Something had forced them up and away from each other, breaking their huddle and good cheer, and introducing them to the true violence and horror of this day. A tall, bald, heavily-scarred man stood turning in the air like heat-haze, swinging an ethereal sword that split a throat, slashed across a bare arm, buried itself in the skull of a short boy.

Lenore heard the screams and shouts but she caught her breath and kept singing. "London Calling," but triple-time now, practically screaming the

words to block out Ellie's haunting tune, that ancient song that kept trying to force its way into her head.

My Ellie, what have you done? she thought, and tears forced against her fear, blurring her vision. It blurred even more when the tall, scarred, ghostly man hacked his way through two terrified boys and came for her.

Still shouting, Lenore tried to gain her feet. Someone knocked her down again—a woman covered in blood trampled across her legs and stomped on her shin. Lenore cried out and kicked against the ground as if to push the whole damned festival away from her, moving backwards as the shape bore down on her. He was tall and imposing and terrible, and she could see through him. He was the most awful, real thing there, yet he was an echo, the roar from his toothless mouth silent, his fury and bloodlust carried and amplified by the persistent sound of Ellie's song.

As the spirit raised his sword, the man who'd been running behind Lenore stepped between him and her.

The spirit paused, weapon raised above and behind him. Then it grinned. It was horrific, filled with so much hate and ferocity that Lenore didn't think she would ever see a smile in the same way again.

The skinny, bearded man took a couple of steps back until he was standing beside where Lenore was still splayed on the ground. They both scrambled further back, moving out of the sword's killing circle.

The man held out his hand. Lenore grabbed hold, let herself be tugged to her feet, and then they were fleeing together, practically flying through the thinning crowd at the outer edge of the song's reach. They started in on "London Calling" again, darting around people who had fallen. Some were gawking, people who'd been on the outskirts or gone to find a bathroom and hadn't yet seen the horror unfolding or been touched by the dark puppetry of Ellie's song. Lenore knew she should warn them, but she and the stranger kept running and soon they were beyond even the last stragglers.

Gasping for breath, heart pounding, she stumbled to a halt and went down on her knees. The guy who'd helped her with his own singing made it a few more steps and then collapsed as well, heaving for air.

Together, catching their breath, they turned to look back the way they'd come. They saw the spirit close his eyes and lower his sword, his grimace settling into a satisfied smile. Then he faded away to nothing.

A dreadful silence settled across the scene, and only then did they realize that Ellie's song had ended. It wasn't that they were too far away to hear it anymore, but that someone had killed the sound system and the amplifiers couldn't reach this far.

Maybe she's stopped singing, Lenore thought.

Grief welled up inside her and she released it in a single, long, keening wail. Pain and anguish tore through her. Maybe Ellie had gone silent because, like so many others, she was dead.

And maybe that was best.

Someone shouted. A man screamed. A woman called a name. And this time without music, and without Ellie's haunting, horrible words, Valhalla began to wake to the sound of a thousand wretched cries.

The stranger stood shakily and came toward Lenore as she did the same. He held her, shaking and seeking solace as well as offering it. Lenore hesitated, then hugged him back.

"We should leave," he said.

"What the fuck happened?"

He didn't answer. She pulled back and looked into his eyes, and behind the reflection of her own horror—and which she saw in the faces of all those around them, in the people just starting to stand, heads shaking, eyes blurred, skin spattered with the blood of loved ones and strangers alike—she saw something else that she also felt. The need for company.

Neither of them could be on their own.

CHAPTER 14 ◆ JOSHUA

They stayed together, taking comfort from each other. Lenore told him she'd lost people. She said it had been her best friend singing that song. Joshua didn't really know what to make of that. There was a lot that confused him. They walked hand in hand beyond the festival site, and when the fleets of ambulances and police cars started to arrive, they joined a large group of people milling about at the foot of Valhalla Hill. It felt natural holding hands, because they both needed the contact. Joshua couldn't imagine being on his own right then.

Time and again he replayed that moment when he'd stood between the vicious Viking ghost and the girl he hadn't known thirty minutes ago. It was a flash of bravery he hadn't known he had inside him, but it was something else as well.

Did I know?

There was no way.

The warrior, dead for a thousand years, murdered by those he had conquered and then slowly grown to trust, had looked into Joshua's eyes and smiled.

And it was like looking into my own eyes.

"Choppers," Lenore said.

"Huh?"

She nodded to the east. Several helicopters were flying in from that direction, the sound growing as they drew closer. More emergency vehicles were arriving by the minute, and as the severity of the incident became more apparent, a sense of underlying panic could be seen in the activities of the police and paramedics. Several armed police units had also arrived, and officers in balaclavas and carrying machine guns patroled the festival's outer boundary. They had no apparent mission in mind. Joshua wasn't certain whether they were keeping people in, or out.

"Everyone's gone," Lenore said.

"Not everyone."

"I saw her cut in half right in front of me." She'd said this a few times already. Someone called Zoe. Joshua didn't know who she was, and knowing wouldn't change anything.

They walked back and forth across the base of the hill, scared to go closer to the festival site, too traumatized to turn away. Joshua felt a powerful draw holding him there, and it was similar to the pull he felt to visit the place every year, whether the Valhalla Festival was taking place or not. Similar to the feeling he'd felt on hearing the strange strains of that unknown song.

Many of the people around them were watching the news on their mobile phones. He heard a slew of familiar terms that always made his stomach drop—*breaking news . . . this just in . . . we interrupt this program*. News of the tragedy at Valhalla was already spreading out into the world, and the people here seemed to be taking more comfort from watching reports on their phones than actually observing what was going on so close to them. Maybe they thought they'd learn more from newscasters in a studio a hundred miles distant. Or perhaps it was simply the comfort of familiarity, and belonging. Grasping onto something they knew, in an effort to escape the existential horror of something they did not.

"I don't know what to do," Lenore said.

"My car's close," Joshua said.

"No. I need to stay here. I need to see if Ellie . . . "

"Ellie who sang that song?" he asked quietly, looking around to make sure no one else heard what they were talking about.

Lenore looked at him, wide-eyed and afraid, because she didn't know what to do. None of them did, and however many police and helicopters and paramedics turned up, he thought it was a feeling that would stay with them both for a long time.

There was a sudden flurry of movement in some of the people around them, and Joshua took in a sharp breath as his heart fluttered. *Not again!* But it was just something some of them had seen on their phones.

Lenore pulled him closer to an elderly couple, sitting in the grass and watching the news on a large phone screen. The picture was blurred, but it only took Joshua a moment to recognise that it was being filmed close to

the Ragnar stage. Press had already found their way into the festival. And it was a disaster.

"I don't know . . ." the reporter said. "If you can see . . . " She kept trailing off, because there was really nothing to be said.

The only people alive in her shaky footage were emergency personnel and police. The image flipped down to her leg several times, as if she was hiding the camera from someone, and Joshua wondered if she was really press at all. Maybe she was a police officer, filming and transmitting this to an outside provider.

There were bodies everywhere. Dead beyond counting. He felt sick looking at it, and knew that by evening this footage would have been edited and made suitable for national broadcast. But he'd already seen enough. He could feel blood drying on his skin.

He turned and went to walk away, but Lenore grabbed his hand and tugged him back.

"Ellie!" she breathed.

At the same moment, the woman filming from inside the festival said, "Here's someone alive! A young woman, covered in blood, she's walking towards me and . . . hey, are you okay? I hope you can all see this. Hey, what's your name? What happened here?"

"Oh, no," Joshua said. Because the girl the camera was now focused on was smiling, and he recognized those eyes.

As she opened her mouth and began to sing, he snatched the phone from the old man's hands, dropped it to the ground, and stomped on it. His hands were shaking. He feared it might have been the beginnings of a dance.

"No, Ellie, no," Lenore said, and she fell to her knees sobbing.

From across the foot of the hillside, the girl started to sing.

Her song went out live, nationwide.

ABOUT THE CREATORS

CHRISTOPHER GOLDEN is the New York Times bestselling, Bram Stoker Award-winning author of such novels as Road of Bones, Ararat, Snowblind, and Red Hands. With Mike Mignola, he is the co-creator of the Outerverse comic book universe, including Baltimore, Joe Golem, and Lady Baltimore. He has also written for film, television, and video games. As an editor, his anthologies include Hex Life, Seize the Night, The New Dead, and others. With Charlaine Harris, he co-wrote the New York Times #1 bestselling graphic novel trilogy, Cemetery Girl. He was born and raised in Massachusetts, where he still lives with his family. His work has been nominated for the British Fantasy Award, the Eisner Award, and multiple Shirley Jackson Awards. For the Bram Stoker Awards, Golden has been nominated ten times in eight different categories, and won twice. His original novels have been published in more than fifteen languages in countries around the world. Please visit him at www.christophergolden.com

◆ ◆ ◆

TIM LEBBON is a New York Times-bestselling writer from South Wales. He's had over forty novels published to date, as well as hundreds of novellas and short stories. His latest novel is the eco-horror The Last Storm. Other recent releases include Eden, The Silence and Blood of the Four with Christopher Golden. He has won four British Fantasy Awards, as well as Bram Stoker, Scribe and Dragon Awards, and has been shortlisted for World Fantasy, International Horror Guild and Shirley Jackson Awards. The movie of his novel The Silence, starring Stanley Tucci and Kiernan Shipka, debuted on Netflix April 2019, and Pay the Ghost, starring Nicolas Cage, was released Hallowe'en 2015. Tim is currently developing more novels, short stories, audio dramas, video games, comics, and projects for TV and the big screen.

◆ ◆ ◆

PETER BERGTING has spent all of his life drawing silly and scary things and made his comic book debut with the 2006 series The Portent. He loves working on his slice of the Mignolaverse and plops down in front of the drawing board with a big, cheesy grin every day.